Owen Wingrave

By

Henry James

British Library Cataloguing-in-Publication Data
A catalogue record for this book is available from the
British Library

Contents

Henry James

Henry James was born in New York City in 1843. One of thirteen children, James had an unorthodox early education, switching between schools, private tutors and private reading. In 1855, the James family embarked on a three year-long trip to Geneva, London, and Paris; an experience that greatly influenced his decision, some years later, to emigrate to Europe. Having returned to America, and having met prominent authors and thinkers such as Ralph Waldo Emerson and Henry David Thoreau, James turned seriously to writing.

James published his first story, 'A Tragedy of Error', in the Continental Monthly in 1864, when he was twenty years old. In 1876, he emigrated to London, where he remained for the vast majority of the rest of his life, becoming a British citizen in 1915. From this point on, he was a hugely prolific author, eventually producing twenty novels and more than a hundred short stories and novellas, as well as literary criticism, plays and travelogues. Amongst James's most famous works are The Europeans (1878), Daisy Miller (1878), Washington Square (1880), The Bostonians (1886), and one of the most famous ghost stories of all time, The Turn of the Screw (1898). James' personal favourite, of all his works, was the 1903 novel The Ambassadors. He is regarded by modern-day critics as one of the key figures of 19th-century literary realism, and one of the greatest American authors of all-time.

James' autobiography appeared in three volumes between 1914 and 1917. He died following a stroke in February of 1916, aged 72.

1

"Upon my honour you must be off your head!" cried Spencer Coyle, as the young man, with a white face, stood there panting a little and repeating "Really, I've quite decided," and "I assure you I've thought it all out." They were both pale, but Owen Wingrave smiled in a manner exasperating to his interlocutor, who however still discriminated sufficiently to see that his grimace (it was like an irrelevant leer) was the result of extreme and conceivable nervousness.

"It was certainly a mistake to have gone so far; but that is exactly why I feel I mustn't go further," poor Owen said, waiting mechanically, almost humbly (he wished not to swagger, and indeed he had nothing to swagger about) and carrying through the window to the stupid opposite houses the dry glitter of his eyes.

"I'm unspeakably disgusted. You've made me dreadfully ill," Mr Coyle went on, looking thoroughly upset.

"I'm very sorry. It was the fear of the effect on you that kept me from speaking sooner."

"You should have spoken three months ago. Don't you know your mind from one day to the other?"

The young man for a moment said nothing. Then he replied with a little tremor: "You're very angry with me, and I expected it. I'm awfully obliged to you for all you've done for me. I'll do anything else for you in return, but I can't do that. Everyone else will let me have it, of course. I'm prepared for it – I'm prepared for everything. That's what has taken the time: to be sure I was prepared. I think it's your displeasure I feel most and regret most. But little by little you'll get over it."

"You'll get over it rather faster, I suppose!" Spencer Coyle satirically exclaimed. He was quite as agitated as his young friend, and they were evidently in no condition to prolong an encounter in which they each drew blood. Mr Coyle was a professional 'coach'; he prepared young men for the army, taking only three or four at a time, to whom he applied the irresistible stimulus of which the possession was both his secret and his fortune. He had not a great establishment; he would have said himself that it was not a wholesale business. Neither his system, his health nor his temper could have accommodated itself to numbers; so he weighed and measured his pupils and turned away more applicants than he passed. He was an artist in his line, caring only for picked subjects and capable of sacrifices almost passionate for the individual. He liked ardent young men (there were kinds of capacity to which he was indifferent) and he had taken a particular fancy to Owen Wingrave. This young man's facility really fascinated him. His candidates usually did wonders, and he might have sent up a multitude. He was a person of exactly the stature of the great Napoleon, with a certain flicker of genius in his light blue eye: it had been said of him that he looked like a pianist. The tone of his favourite pupil now expressed, without intention indeed, a superior wisdom which irritated him. He had not especially suffered before from Wingrave's high opinion of himself, which had seemed justified by remarkable parts; but to-day it struck him as intolerable. He cut short the discussion, declining absolutely to regard their relations as terminated, and remarked to his pupil that he had better go off somewhere (down to Eastbourne, say; the sea would bring him round) and take a few days to find his feet and come to his senses. He could afford the time, he was so well up: when Spencer Coyle remembered how well up he was he could have boxed his ears. The tall, athletic young man was not physically a subject for simplified reasoning; but there was a troubled gentleness in his handsome face, the index of compunction mixed with pertinacity, which signified that if it could have done any good he would have turned both cheeks. He evidently didn't pretend that his wisdom was superior; he only presented it as his own. It was his own career after all that was in question. He couldn't refuse to go through the form of trying Eastbourne or at least of holding his tongue, though there was that in his manner which implied that if he should do so it would be really to give Mr Coyle a chance to recuperate. He didn't feel a bit overworked, but there was nothing more natural than that with their tremendous pressure Mr Coyle should be. Mr Coyle's own intellect would derive an advantage from his pupil's holiday. Mr Coyle saw what he meant, but he controlled himself; he only demanded, as his right, a truce of three days. Owen Wingrave granted it, though as fostering sad illusions this went visibly against his conscience; but before they separated the famous crammer remarked:

"All the same I feel as if I ought to see someone. I think

you mentioned to me that your aunt had come to town?"

"Oh yes; she's in Baker Street. Do go and see her," the boy said comfortingly.

Mr Coyle looked at him an instant. "Have you broached this folly to her?"

"Not yet – to no one. I thought it right to speak to you first."

"Oh, what you 'think right'!" cried Spencer Coyle, outraged by his young friend's standards. He added that he would probably call on Miss Wingrave; after which the recreant youth got out of the house.

Owen Wingrave didn't however start punctually for Eastbourne; he only directed his steps to Kensington Gardens, from which Mr Coyle's desirable residence (he was terribly expensive and had a big house) was not far removed. The famous coach 'put up' his pupils, and Owen had mentioned to the butler that he would be back to dinner. The spring day was warm to his young blood, and he had a book in his pocket which, when he had passed into the gardens and, after a short stroll, dropped into a chair, he took out with the slow, soft sigh that finally ushers in a pleasure postponed. He stretched his long legs and began to read it; it was a volume of Goethe's poems. He had been for days in a state of the highest tension, and now that the cord had snapped the relief was proportionate; only it was characteristic of him that this deliverance should take the form of an intellectual pleasure. If he had thrown up the probability of a magnificent career it was not to dawdle along Bond Street nor parade his indifference in the window of a club. At any rate he had in a few moments forgotten everything – the tremendous pressure, Mr Coyle's disappointment, and even his formidable aunt in Baker Street. If these watchers had overtaken him there would surely have been some excuse for their exasperation. There was no doubt he was perverse, for his very choice of a pastime only showed how he had got up his German.

"What the devil's the matter with him, do you know?" Spencer Coyle asked that afternoon of young Lechmere, who had never before observed the head of the establishment to set a fellow such an example of bad language. Young Lechmere was not only Wingrave's fellow-pupil, he was supposed to be his intimate, indeed quite his best friend, and had unconsciously performed for Mr Coyle the office of making the promise of his great gifts more vivid by contrast. He was short and sturdy and as a general thing uninspired, and Mr Coyle, who found no amusement in believing in him, had never thought him less exciting than as he stared now out of a face from which you could never guess whether he had caught an idea. Young Lechmere concealed such achievements as if they had been youthful indiscretions. At any rate he could evidently conceive no reason why it should be thought there was anything more than usual the matter with the companion of his studies; so Mr Coyle had to continue:

"He declines to go up. He chucks the whole thing!"

The first thing that struck young Lechmere in the case was

the freshness it had imparted to the governor's vocabulary.

"He doesn't want to go to Sandhurst?"

"He doesn't want to go anywhere. He gives up the army altogether. He objects," said Mr Coyle, in a tone that made young Lechmere almost hold his breath, "to the military profession."

"Why, it has been the profession of all his family!"

"Their profession? It has been their religion! Do you know Miss Wingrave?"

"Oh, yes. Isn't she awful?" young Lechmere candidly ejaculated.

His instructor demurred.

"She's formidable, if you mean that, and it's right she should be; because somehow in her very person, good maiden lady as she is, she represents the might, she represents the traditions and the exploits of the British army. She represents the expansive property of the English name. I think his family can be trusted to come down on him, but every influence should be set in motion. I want to know what yours is. Can you do anything in the matter?"

"I can try a couple of rounds with him," said young Lechmere reflectively. "But he knows a fearful lot. He has the most extraordinary ideas."

"Then he has told you some of them – he has taken you into his confidence?"

"I've heard him jaw by the yard," smiled the honest youth. "He has told me he despises it."

"What is it he despises? I can't make out."

The most consecutive of Mr Coyle's nurslings considered a moment, as if he were conscious of a responsibility.

"Why, I think, military glory. He says we take the wrong view of it."

"He oughtn't to talk to you that way. It's corrupting the youth of Athens. It's sowing sedition."

"Oh, I'm all right!" said young Lechmere. "And he never told me he meant to chuck it. I always thought he meant to see it through, simply because he had to. He'll argue on any side you like. It's a tremendous pity – I'm sure he'd have a big career."

"Tell him so, then; plead with him; struggle with him – for God's sake."

"I'll do what I can – I'll tell him it's a regular shame."

"Yes, strike that note – insist on the disgrace of it."

The young man gave Mr Coyle a more perceptive glance. "I'm sure he wouldn't do anything dishonourable."

"Well – it won't look right. He must be made to feel that – work it up. Give him a comrade's point of view – that of a brother-in-arms."

"That's what I thought we were going to be!" young Lechmere mused romantically, much uplifted by the nature of the mission imposed on him. "He's an awfully good sort."

"No one will think so if he backs out!" said Spencer Coyle.

"They mustn't say it to me!" his pupil rejoined with a flush.

Mr Coyle hesitated a moment, noting his tone and aware that in the perversity of things, though this young man was a born soldier, no excitement would ever attach to his alternatives save perhaps on the part of the nice girl to whom at an early day he was sure to be placidly united. "Do you like him very much – do you believe in him?"

Young Lechmere's life in these days was spent in answering terrible questions; but he had never been subjected to so queer an interrogation as this. "Believe in him? Rather!"

"Then save him!"

The poor boy was puzzled, as if it were forced upon him by this intensity that there was more in such an appeal than could appear on the surface; and he doubtless felt that he was only entering into a complex situation when after another moment, with his hands in his pockets, he replied hopefully but not pompously: "I daresay I can bring him round!"

2

Before seeing young Lechmere Mr Coyle had determined to telegraph an inquiry to Miss Wingrave. He had prepaid the answer, which, being promptly put into his hand, brought the interview we have just related to a close. He immediately drove off to Baker Street, where the lady had said she awaited him, and five minutes after he got there, as he sat with Owen Wingrave's remarkable aunt, he repeated over several times, in his angry sadness and with the infallibility of his experience: "He's so intelligent – he's so intelligent!" He had declared it had been a luxury to put such a fellow through.

"Of course he's intelligent, what else could he be? We've never, that I know of, had but one idiot in the family!" said Jane Wingrave. This was an allusion that Mr Coyle could understand, and it brought home to him another of the reasons for the disappointment, the humiliation as it were, of the good people at Paramore, at the same time that it gave an example of the conscientious coarseness he had on former occasions observed in his interlocutress. Poor Philip Wingrave, her late brother's eldest son, was literally imbecile and banished from view; deformed, unsocial, irretrievable, he had been relegated to a private asylum and had become among the friends of the family only a little hushed lugubrious legend. All the hopes of the house, picturesque Paramore, now unintermittently old Sir Philip's rather melancholy home (his infirmities would keep him there to the last) were therefore collected on the second boy's head, which nature, as if in compunction for her previous botch, had, in addition to making it strikingly handsome, filled with marked originalities and talents. These two had been the only children of the old man's only son, who, like so many of his ancestors, had given up a gallant young life to the service of his country. Owen Wingrave the elder had received his death-cut, in close-quarters, from an Afghan sabre; the blow had come crashing across his skull. His wife, at that time in India, was about to give birth to her third child; and when the event took place, in darkness and anguish, the baby came lifeless into the world and the mother sank under the multiplication of her woes. The second of the little boys in England, who was at Paramore with his grandfather, became the peculiar charge of his aunt, the only unmarried one, and during the interesting Sunday that, by urgent invitation, Spencer Coyle, busy as he was, had, after consenting to put Owen through, spent under that roof, the celebrated crammer received a vivid impression of the influence exerted at least in intention by Miss Wingrave. Indeed the picture of this short visit remained with the observant little man a curious one – the vision of an impoverished Jacobean house, shabby and remarkably 'creepy', but full of character still and full of felicity as a setting for the distinguished figure of the peaceful old soldier. Sir Philip Wingrave, a relic rather than a celebrity, was a small brown, erect octogenarian, with smouldering eyes and a studied courtesy. He liked to do the diminished honours of his house, but even when with a shaky hand he lighted a bedroom candle for a deprecating guest it was impossible not to feel that beneath the surface he was a merciless old warrior. The eye of the imagination could glance back into his crowded Eastern past – back at episodes in which his scrupulous forms would only have made him more terrible.

Mr Coyle remembered also two other figures – a faded inoffensive Mrs Julian, domesticated there by a system of frequent visits as the widow of an officer and a particular friend of Miss Wingrave, and a remarkably clever little girl of eighteen, who was this lady's daughter and who struck the speculative visitor as already formed for other relations. She was very impertinent to Owen, and in the course of a long walk that he had taken with the young man and the effect of which, in much talk, had been to clinch his high opinion of him, he had learned (for Owen chattered confidentially) that Mrs Julian was the sister of a very gallant gentleman, Captain Hume-Walker, of the Artillery, who had fallen in the Indian Mutiny and between whom and Miss Wingrave (it had been that lady's one known concession) a passage of some delicacy, taking a tragic turn, was believed to have been enacted. They had been engaged to be married, but she had given way to the jealousy of her nature – had broken with him and sent him off to his fate, which had been horrible. A passionate sense of having wronged him, a hard eternal remorse had thereupon taken possession of her, and when his poor sister, linked also to a soldier, had by a still heavier blow been left almost without resources, she had devoted herself charitably to a long expiation. She had sought comfort in taking Mrs Julian to live much of the time at Paramore, where she became an unremunerated though not uncriticised housekeeper, and Spencer Coyle suspected that it was a part of this comfort that she could at her leisure trample on her. The impression of Jane Wingrave was not the faintest he had gathered on that intensifying Sunday – an occasion singularly tinged for him with the sense of bereavement and mourning and memory, of names never mentioned of the far-away plaint of widows and the echoes of battles and bad news. It was all military indeed, and Mr Coyle was made to shudder a little at the profession of which he helped to open the door to harmless young men. Miss Wingrave moreover might have made such a bad conscience worse – so cold and clear a good one looked at him out of her hard, fine eyes and trumpeted in her sonorous voice.

She was a high, distinguished person; angular but not awkward, with a large forehead and abundant black hair, arranged like that of a woman conceiving perhaps excusably of her head as 'noble', and irregularly streaked to-day with white. If however she represented for Spencer Coyle the genius of a military race it was not that she had the step of a grenadier or the vocabulary of a camp-follower; it was only that such sympathies were vividly implied in the general fact to which her very presence and each of her actions and glances and tones were a constant and direct allusion – the paramount valour of her family. If she was military it was because she sprang from a military house and because she wouldn't for the world have been anything but what the Wingraves had been. She was almost vulgar about her ancestors, and if one had been tempted to quarrel with her one would have found a fair pretext in her defective sense of proportion. This temptation however said nothing to Spencer Coyle, for whom as a strong character revealing itself in colour and sound she was a spectacle and who was glad to regard her as a force exerted on his own side. He wished her nephew had more of her narrowness instead of being almost cursed with the tendency to look at things in their relations. He wondered why when she came up to town she always resorted to Baker Street for lodgings. He had never known nor heard of Baker Street as a residence – he associated it only with bazaars and photographers. He divined in her a rigid indifference to everything that was not the passion of her life. Nothing really mattered to her but that, and she would have occupied apartments in Whitechapel if they had been a feature in her tactics. She had received her visitor in a large, cold, faded room, furnished with slippery seats and decorated with alabaster vases and wax-flowers. The only little personal comfort for which she appeared to have looked out was a fat catalogue of the Army and Navy Stores, which reposed on a vast, desolate table-cover of false blue. Her clear forehead – it was like a porcelain slate, a receptacle for addresses and sums – had flushed when her nephew's crammer told her the extraordinary news; but he saw she was fortunately more angry than frightened. She had essentially, she would always have, too little imagination for fear, and the healthy habit moreover of facing everything had taught her that the occasion usually found her a quantity to reckon with. Mr Coyle saw that her only fear at present could have been that of not being able to prevent her nephew from being absurd and that to such an apprehension as this she was in fact inaccessible. Practically too she was not troubled by surprise; she recognised none of the futile, none of the subtle sentiments. If Philip had for an hour made a fool of himself she was angry; disconcerted as she would have been on learning that he had confessed to debts or fallen in love with a low girl. But there remained in any annoyance the saving fact that no one could make a fool of her.

"I don't know when I've taken such an interest in a young man – I think I never have, since I began to handle them," Mr Coyle said. "I like him, I believe in him – it's been a delight to see how he was going."

"Oh, I know how they go!" Miss Wingrave threw back her head with a familiar briskness, as if a rapid procession of the generations had flashed before her, rattling their scabbards and spurs. Spencer Coyle recognised the intimation that she had nothing to learn from anybody about the natural carriage of a Wingrave, and he even felt convicted by her next words of being, in her eyes, with the troubled story of his check, his weak complaint of his pupil, rather a poor creature. "If you like him," she exclaimed, "for mercy's sake keep him quiet!"

Mr Coyle began to explain to her that this was less easy than she appeared to imagine; but he perceived that she understood very little of what he said. The more he insisted that the boy had a kind of intellectual independence, the more this struck her as a conclusive proof that her nephew was a Wingrave and a soldier. It was not till he mentioned to her that Owen had spoken of the profession of arms as of something that would be 'beneath' him, it was not till her attention was arrested by this intenser light on the complexity of the problem that Miss Wingrave broke out after a moment's stupefied reflection: "Send him to see me immediately!"

"That's exactly what I wanted to ask your leave to do. But I've wanted also to prepare you for the worst, to make you understand that he strikes me as really obstinate and to suggest to you that the most powerful arguments at your command – especially if you should be able to put your hand on some intensely practical one – will be none too effective."

"I think I've got a powerful argument." Miss Wingrave looked very hard at her visitor. He didn't know in the least what it was, but he begged her to put it forward without delay. He promised that their young man should come to Baker Street that evening, mentioning however that he had already urged him to spend without delay a couple of days at Eastbourne. This led Jane Wingrave to inquire with surprise what virtue there might be in that expensive remedy, and to reply with decision when Mr Coyle had said "The virtue of a little rest, a little change, a little relief to overwrought nerves," "Ah, don't coddle him – he's costing us a great deal of money! I'll talk to him and I'll take him down to Paramore; then I'll send him back to you straightened out."

Spencer Coyle hailed this pledge superficially with

satisfaction, but before he quitted Miss Wingrave he became conscious that he had really taken on a new anxiety – a restlessness that made him say to himself, groaning inwardly: 'Oh, she is a grenadier at bottom, and she'll have no tact. I don't know what her powerful argument is; I'm only afraid she'll be stupid and make him worse. The old man's better – he's capable of tact, though he's not quite an extinct volcano. Owen will probably put him in a rage. In short the difficulty is that the boy's the best of them.'

Spencer Coyle felt afresh that evening at dinner that the boy was the best of them. Young Wingrave (who, he was pleased to observe, had not yet proceeded to the seaside) appeared at the repast as usual, looking inevitably a little self-conscious, but not too original for Bayswater. He talked very naturally to Mrs Coyle, who had thought him from the first the most beautiful young man they had ever received; so that the person most ill at ease was poor Lechmere, who took great trouble, as if from the deepest delicacy, not to meet the eye of his misguided mate. Spencer Coyle however paid the penalty of his own profundity in feeling more and more worried; he could so easily see that there were all sorts of things in his young friend that the people of Paramore wouldn't understand. He began even already to react against the notion of his being harassed – to reflect that after all he had a right to his ideas – to remember that he was of a substance too fine to be in fairness roughly used. It was in this way that the ardent little crammer, with his whimsical perceptions and complicated sympathies, was generally condemned not to settle down comfortably either into his displeasures or into his enthusiasms. His love of the real truth never gave him a chance to enjoy them. He mentioned to Wingrave after dinner the propriety of an immediate visit to Baker Street, and the young man, looking 'queer', as he thought – that is smiling again with the exaggerated glory he had shown in their recent interview – went off to face the ordeal. Spencer Coyle noted that he was scared – he was afraid of his aunt; but somehow this didn't strike him as a sign of pusillanimity. He should have been scared, he was well aware, in the poor boy's place, and the sight of his pupil marching up to the battery in spite of his terrors was a positive suggestion of the temperament of the soldier. Many a plucky youth would have shirked this particular peril.

"He has got ideas!" young Lechmere broke out to his instructor after his comrade had quitted the house. He was evidently bewildered and agitated – he had an emotion to work off. He had before dinner gone straight at his friend, as Mr Coyle had requested, and had elicited from him that his scruples were founded on an overwhelming conviction of the stupidity – the 'crass barbarism' he called it – of war. His great complaint was that people hadn't invented anything cleverer, and he was determined to show, the only way he could, that he wasn't such an ass.

"And he thinks all the great generals ought to have been shot, and that Napoleon Bonaparte in particular, the greatest, was a criminal, a monster for whom language has no adequate name!" Mr Coyle rejoined, completing young

Lechmere's picture. "He favoured you, I see, with exactly the same pearls of wisdom that he produced for me. But I want to know what you said."

"I said they were awful rot!" Young Lechmere spoke with emphasis, and he was slightly surprised to hear Mr Coyle laugh incongruously at this just declaration and then after a moment continue:

"It's all very curious – I daresay there's something in it. But it's a pity!"

"He told me when it was that the question began to strike him in that light. Four or five years ago, when he did a lot of reading about all the great swells and their campaigns – Hannibal and Julius Cæsar, Marlborough and Frederick and Bonaparte. He has done a lot of reading, and he says it opened his eyes. He says that a wave of disgust rolled over him. He talked about the 'immeasurable misery' of wars, and asked me why nations don't tear to pieces the governments, the rulers that go in for them. He hates poor old Bonaparte worst of all."

"Well, poor old Bonaparte was a brute. He was a frightful ruffian," Mr Coyle unexpectedly declared. "But I suppose you didn't admit that."

"Oh, I daresay he was objectionable, and I'm very glad we laid him on his back. But the point I made to Wingrave was that his own behaviour would excite no end of remark." Young Lechmere hesitated an instant, then he added: "I told him he must be prepared for the worst."

"Of course he asked you what you meant by the 'worst',"

said Spencer Coyle.

"Yes, he asked me that, and do you know what I said? I said people would say that his conscientious scruples and his wave of disgust are only a pretext. Then he asked 'A pretext for what?'"

"Ah, he rather had you there!" Mr Coyle exclaimed with a little laugh that was mystifying to his pupil.

"Not a bit – for I told him."

"What did you tell him?"

Once more, for a few seconds, with his conscious eyes in his instructor's, the young man hung fire.

"Why, what we spoke of a few hours ago. The appearance he'd present of not having—" The honest youth faltered a moment, then brought it out: "The military temperament, don't you know? But do you know what he said to that?" young Lechmere went on.

"Damn the military temperament!" the crammer promptly replied.

Young Lechmere stared. Mr Coyle's tone left him uncertain if he were attributing the phrase to Wingrave or uttering his own opinion, but he exclaimed:

"Those were exactly his words!"

"He doesn't care," said Mr Coyle.

"Perhaps not. But it isn't fair for him to abuse us fellows. I told him it's the finest temperament in the world, and that there's nothing so splendid as pluck and heroism."

"Ah! there you had him."

"I told him it was unworthy of him to abuse a gallant, a

magnificent profession. I told him there's no type so fine as that of the soldier doing his duty."

"That's essentially your type, my dear boy." Young Lechmere blushed; he couldn't make out (and the danger was naturally unexpected to him) whether at that moment he didn't exist mainly for the recreation of his friend. But he was partly reassured by the genial way this friend continued, laying a hand on his shoulder: "Keep at him that way! we may do something. I'm extremely obliged to you." Another doubt however remained unassuaged – a doubt which led him to exclaim to Mr Coyle before they dropped the painful subject:

"He doesn't care! But it's awfully odd he shouldn't!"

"So it is, but remember what you said this afternoon – I mean about your not advising people to make insinuations to you."

"I believe I should knock a fellow down!" said young Lechmere. Mr Coyle had got up; the conversation had taken place while they sat together after Mrs Coyle's withdrawal from the dinner-table and the head of the establishment administered to his disciple, on principles that were a part of his thoroughness, a glass of excellent claret. The disciple, also on his feet, lingered an instant, not for another 'go', as he would have called it, at the decanter, but to wipe his microscopic moustache with prolonged and unusual care. His companion saw he had something to bring out which required a final effort, and waited for him an instant with a hand on the knob of the door. Then as young Lechmere approached him Spencer Coyle grew conscious of an unwonted intensity in the round and ingenuous face. The boy was nervous, but he tried to behave like a man of the world. "Of course, it's between ourselves," he stammered, "and I wouldn't breathe such a word to any one who wasn't interested in poor Wingrave as you are. But do you think he funks it?"

Mr Coyle looked at him so hard for an instant that he was visibly frightened at what he had said.

"Funks it! Funks what?"

"Why, what we're talking about – the service." Young Lechmere gave a little gulp and added with a naïveté almost pathetic to Spencer Coyle: "The dangers, you know!"

"Do you mean he's thinking of his skin?"

Young Lechmere's eyes expanded appealingly, and what his instructor saw in his pink face – he even thought he saw a tear – was the dread of a disappointment shocking in the degree in which the loyalty of admiration had been great.

"Is he – is he afraid?" repeated the honest lad, with a quaver of suspense.

"Dear no!" said Spencer Coyle, turning his back.

Young Lechmere felt a little snubbed and even a little ashamed; but he felt still more relieved.

3

Less than a week after this Spencer Coyle received a note from Miss Wingrave, who had immediately quitted London with her nephew. She proposed that he should come down to Paramore for the following Sunday – Owen was really so tiresome. On the spot, in that house of examples and memories and in combination with her poor dear father, who was 'dreadfully annoyed', it might be worth their while to make a last stand. Mr Coyle read between the lines of this letter that the party at Paramore had got over a good deal of ground since Miss Wingrave, in Baker Street, had treated his despair as superficial. She was not an insinuating woman, but she went so far as to put the question on the ground of his conferring a particular favour on an afflicted family; and she expressed the pleasure it would give them if he should be accompanied by Mrs Coyle, for whom she inclosed a separate invitation. She mentioned that she was also writing, subject to Mr Coyle's approval, to young Lechmere. She thought such a nice manly boy might do her wretched nephew some good. The celebrated crammer determined to embrace this opportunity; and now it was the case not so much that he was angry as that he was anxious. As he directed his answer to Miss Wingrave's letter he caught himself smiling at the thought that at bottom he was going to defend his young friend rather than to attack him. He said to his wife, who was a fair, fresh, slow woman – a person of much more presence than himself – that she had better take Miss Wingrave at her word: it was such an extraordinary, such a fascinating specimen of an old English home. This last allusion was amicably sarcastic – he had already accused the good lady more than once of being in love with Owen Wingrave. She admitted that she was, she even gloried in her passion; which shows that the subject, between them, was treated in a liberal spirit. She carried out the joke by accepting the invitation with eagerness. Young Lechmere was delighted to do the same; his instructor had good-naturedly taken the view that the little break would freshen him up for his last spurt.

It was the fact that the occupants of Paramore did indeed take their trouble hard that struck Spencer Coyle after he had been an hour or two in that fine old house. This very short second visit, beginning on the Saturday evening, was to constitute the strangest episode of his life. As soon as he found himself in private with his wife – they had retired to dress for dinner – they called each other's attention with effusion and almost with alarm to the sinister gloom that was stamped on the place. The house was admirable with its old grey front which came forward in wings so as to form three sides of a square, but Mrs Coyle made no scruple to declare that if she had known in advance the sort of impression she was going to receive she would never have put her foot in it. She characterized it as 'uncanny', she accused her husband of not having warned her properly. He had mentioned to her in advance certain facts, but while she almost feverishly dressed she had innumerable questions to ask. He hadn't told her about the girl, the extraordinary girl, Miss Julian – that is, he hadn't told her that this young lady, who in plain terms was a mere dependent, would be in effect, and as a consequence of the way she carried herself, the most important person in the house. Mrs Coyle was already prepared to announce that she hated Miss Julian's affectations. Her husband above all hadn't told her that they should find their young charge looking five years older.

"I couldn't imagine that," said Mr Coyle, "nor that the character of the crisis here would be quite so perceptible. But I suggested to Miss Wingrave the other day that they should press her nephew in real earnest, and she has taken me at my word. They've cut off his supplies – they're trying to starve him out. That's not what I meant – but indeed I don't quite know to-day what I meant. Owen feels the pressure, but he won't yield." The strange thing was that, now that he was there, the versatile little coach felt still more that his own spirit had been caught up by a wave of reaction. If he was there it was because he was on poor Owen's side. His whole impression, his whole apprehension, had on the spot become much deeper. There was something in the dear boy's very resistance that began to charm him. When his wife, in the intimacy of the conference I have mentioned, threw off the mask and commended even with extravagance the stand his pupil had taken (he was too good to be a horrid soldier and it was noble of him to suffer for his convictions – wasn't he as upright as a young hero, even though as pale as a Christian martyr?) the good lady only expressed the sympathy which, under cover of regarding his young friend as a rare exception, he had already recognised in his own soul.

For, half an hour ago, after they had had superficial tea in the brown old hall of the house, his young friend had proposed to him, before going to dress, to take a turn outside, and had even, on the terrace, as they walked together to one of the far ends of it, passed his hand entreatingly into his companion's arm, permitting himself thus a familiarity unusual between pupil and master and calculated to show that he had guessed whom he could most depend on to be kind to him. Spencer Coyle on his own side had guessed something, so that he was not surprised at the boy's having a particular confidence to make. He had felt on arriving that each member of the party had wished to get hold of him first, and he knew that at that moment Jane Wingrave was peering through the ancient blur of one of the windows (the house had been modernised so little that the thick dim panes were three centuries old) to see if her nephew looked as if he were poisoning the visitor's mind. Mr Coyle lost no time therefore in reminding the youth (and he took care to laugh as he did so) that he had not come down to Paramore to be corrupted. He had come down to make, face to face, a last appeal to him – he hoped it wouldn't be utterly vain. Owen smiled sadly as they went, asking him if he thought he had the general air of a fellow who was going to knock under.

"I think you look strange – I think you look ill," Spencer Coyle said very honestly. They had paused at the end of the terrace.

"I've had to exercise a great power of resistance, and it

rather takes it out of one."

"Ah, my dear boy, I wish your great power – for you evidently possess it – were exerted in a better cause!"

Owen Wingrave smiled down at his small instructor. "I don't believe that!" Then he added, to explain why: "Isn't what you want, if you're so good as to think well of my character, to see me exert most power, in whatever direction? Well, this is the way I exert most." Owen Wingrave went on to relate that he had had some terrible hours with his grandfather, who had denounced him in a way to make one's hair stand up on one's head. He had expected them not to like it, not a bit, but he had had no idea they would make such a row. His aunt was different, but she was equally insulting. Oh, they had made him feel they were ashamed of him; they accused him of putting a public dishonour on their name. He was the only one who had ever backed out – he was the first for three hundred years. Every one had known he was to go up, and now every one would know he was a young hypocrite who suddenly pretended to have scruples. They talked of his scruples as you wouldn't talk of a cannibal's god. His grandfather had called him outrageous names. "He called me – he called me—" Here the young man faltered, his voice failed him. He looked as haggard as was possible to a young man in such magnificent health.

"I probably know!" said Spencer Coyle, with a nervous laugh.

Owen Wingrave's clouded eyes, as if they were following the far-off consequences of things, rested for an instant on a distant object. Then they met his companion's and for another moment sounded them deeply. "It isn't true. No, it isn't. It's not that!"

"I don't suppose it is! But what do you propose instead of it?"

"Instead of what?"

"Instead of the stupid solution of war. If you take that away you should suggest at least a substitute."

"That's for the people in charge, for governments and cabinets," said Owen Wingrave. "They'll arrive soon enough at a substitute, in the particular case, if they're made to understand that they'll be hung if they don't find one. Make it a capital crime – that'll quicken the wits of ministers!" His eyes brightened as he spoke, and he looked assured and exalted. Mr Coyle gave a sigh of perplexed resignation – it was a monomania. He fancied after this for a moment that Owen was going to ask him if he too thought he was a coward; but he was relieved to observe that he either didn't suspect him of it or shrank uncomfortably from putting the question to the test. Spencer Coyle wished to show confidence, but somehow a direct assurance that he didn't doubt of his courage appeared too gross a compliment – it would be like saying he didn't doubt of his honesty. The difficulty was presently averted by Owen's continuing: "My grandfather can't break the entail, but I shall have nothing but this place, which, as you know, is small and, with the way rents are going, has quite ceased to yield an income. He has some money – not much, but such as it is he cuts me off. My aunt does the same – she has let me know her intentions. She was to have left me her six hundred a year. It was all settled; but now what's settled is that I don't get a penny of it if I give up the army. I must add in fairness that I have from my mother three hundred a year of my own. And I tell you the simple truth when I say that I don't care a rap for the loss of the money." The young man drew a long, slow breath, like a creature in pain; then he subjoined: "That's not what worries me!"

"What are you going to do?" asked Spencer Coyle.

"I don't know; perhaps nothing. Nothing great, at all events. Only something peaceful!"

Owen gave a weary smile, as if, worried as he was, he could yet appreciate the humorous effect of such a declaration from a Wingrave; but what it suggested to his companion, who looked up at him with a sense that he was after all not a Wingrave for nothing and had a military steadiness under fire, was the exasperation that such a programme, uttered in such a way and striking them as the last word of the inglorious, might well have engendered on the part of his grandfather and his aunt. 'Perhaps nothing' – when he might carry on the great tradition! Yes, he wasn't weak, and he was interesting; but there was a point of view from which he was provoking. "What is it then that worries you?" Mr Coyle demanded.

"Oh, the house – the very air and feeling of it. There are strange voices in it that seem to mutter at me – to say dreadful things as I pass. I mean the general consciousness and responsibility of what I'm doing. Of course it hasn't been easy for me – not a bit. I assure you I don't enjoy it." With a light in them that was like a longing for justice Owen again bent his eyes on those of the little coach; then he pursued: "I've started up all the old ghosts. The very portraits glower at me on the walls. There's one of my great-great-grandfather (the one the extraordinary story you know is about – the old fellow who hangs on the second landing of the big staircase) that fairly stirs on the canvas – just heaves a little – when I come near it. I have to go up and down stairs – it's rather awkward! It's what my aunt calls the family circle. It's all constituted here, it's a kind of indestructible presence, it stretches away into the past, and when I came back with her the other day Miss Wingrave told me I wouldn't have the impudence to stand in the midst of it and say such things. I had to say them to my grandfather; but now that I've said them it seems to me that the question's ended. I want to go away – I don't care if I never come back again."

"Oh, you are a soldier; you must fight it out!" Mr Coyle laughed.

The young man seemed discouraged at his levity, but as they turned round, strolling back in the direction from which they had come, he himself smiled faintly after an instant and replied:

"Ah, we're tainted – all!"

They walked in silence part of the way to the old portico; then Spencer Coyle, stopping short after having assured himself that he was at a sufficient distance from the house not to be heard, suddenly put the question: "What does Miss Julian say?"

"Miss Julian?" Owen had perceptibly coloured.

"I'm sure she hasn't concealed her opinion."

"Oh, it's the opinion of the family circle, for she's a member of it of course. And then she has her own as well."

"Her own opinion?"

"Her own family-circle."

"Do you mean her mother – that patient lady?"

"I mean more particularly her father, who fell in battle. And her grandfather, and his father, and her uncles and great-uncles – they all fell in battle."

"Hasn't the sacrifice of so many lives been sufficient? Why should she sacrifice you?"

"Oh, she hates me!" Owen declared, as they resumed their walk.

"Ah, the hatred of pretty girls for fine young men!" exclaimed Spencer Coyle.

He didn't believe in it, but his wife did, it appeared perfectly, when he mentioned this conversation while, in the fashion that has been described, the visitors dressed for dinner. Mrs Coyle had already discovered that nothing could have been nastier than Miss Julian's manner to the disgraced youth during the half-hour the party had spent in the hall; and it was this lady's judgment that one must have had no eyes in one's head not to see that she was already trying outrageously to flirt with young Lechmere. It was a pity they had brought that silly boy: he was down in the hall with her at that moment. Spencer Coyle's version was different; he thought there were finer elements involved. The girl's footing in the house was inexplicable on any ground save that of her being predestined to Miss Wingrave's nephew. As the niece of Miss Wingrave's own unhappy intended she had been dedicated early by this lady to the office of healing by a union with Owen the tragic breach that had separated their elders; and if in reply to this it was to be said that a girl of spirit couldn't enjoy in such a matter having her duty cut out for her, Owen's enlightened friend was ready with the argument that a young person in Miss Julian's position would never be such a fool as really to quarrel with a capital chance. She was familiar at Paramore and she felt safe; therefore she might trust herself to the amusement of pretending that she had her option. But it was all innocent coquetry. She had a curious charm, and it was vain to pretend that the heir of that house wouldn't seem good enough to a girl, clever as she might be, of eighteen. Mrs Coyle reminded her husband that the poor young man was precisely now not of that house: this problem was among the questions that exercised their wits after the two men had taken the turn on the terrace. Spencer Coyle told his wife that Owen was afraid of the portrait of his great-great-grandfather. He would show it to her, since she hadn't noticed it, on their way down stairs.

"Why of his great-great-grandfather more than of any of the others?"

"Oh, because he's the most formidable. He's the one who's sometimes seen."

"Seen where?" Mrs Coyle had turned round with a jerk.

"In the room he was found dead in – the White Room they've always called it."

"Do you mean to say the house has a ghost?" Mrs Coyle almost shrieked. "You brought me here without telling me?"

"Didn't I mention it after my other visit?"

"Not a word. You only talked about Miss Wingrave."

"Oh, I was full of the story – you have simply forgotten."

"Then you should have reminded me!"

"If I had thought of it I would have held my peace, for you wouldn't have come."

"I wish, indeed, I hadn't!" cried Mrs Coyle. "What is the story?"

"Oh, a deed of violence that took place here ages ago. I think it was in George the First's time. Colonel Wingrave, one of their ancestors, struck in a fit of passion one of his children, a lad just growing up, a blow on the head of which the unhappy child died. The matter was hushed up for the hour – some other explanation was put about. The poor boy was laid out in one of those rooms on the other side of the house, and amid strange smothered rumours the funeral was hurried on. The next morning, when the household assembled, Colonel Wingrave was missing; he was looked for vainly, and at last it occurred to some one that he might perhaps be in the room from which his child had been carried to burial. The seeker knocked without an answer – then opened the door. Colonel Wingrave lay dead on the floor, in his clothes, as if he had reeled and fallen back, without a wound, without a mark, without anything in his appearance to indicate that he had either struggled or suffered. He was a strong, sound man – there was nothing to account for such a catastrophe. He is supposed to have gone to the room during the night, just before going to bed, in some fit of compunction or some fascination of dread. It was only after this that the truth about the boy came out. But no one ever sleeps in the room."

Mrs Coyle had fairly turned pale. "I hope not! Thank heaven they haven't put us there!"

"We're at a comfortable distance; but I've seen the gruesome chamber."

"Do you mean you've been in it?"

"For a few moments. They're rather proud of it and my young friend showed it to me when I was here before."

Mrs Coyle stared. "And what is it like?"

"Simply like an empty, dull, old-fashioned bedroom, rather big, with the things of the 'period' in it. It's panelled from floor to ceiling, and the panels evidently, years and years ago, were painted white. But the paint has darkened with time and there are three or four quaint little ancient 'samplers', framed and glazed, hung on the walls."

Mrs Coyle looked round with a shudder. "I'm glad there are no samplers here! I never heard anything so jumpy! Come down to dinner."

On the staircase as they went down her husband showed her the portrait of Colonel Wingrave – rather a vigorous representation, for the place and period, of a gentleman with a hard, handsome face, in a red coat and a peruke. Mrs Coyle declared that his descendant Sir Philip was wonderfully like him; and her husband could fancy, though he kept it to himself, that if one should have the courage to walk about the old corridors of Paramore at night one might meet a figure that resembled him roaming, with the restlessness of a ghost, hand in hand with the figure of a tall boy. As he proceeded to the drawing-room with his wife he found himself suddenly wishing that he had made more of a point of his pupil's going to Eastbourne. The evening however seemed to have taken upon itself to dissipate any such whimsical forebodings, for the grimness of the family-circle, as Spencer Coyle had preconceived its composition, was mitigated by an infusion of the 'neighbourhood'. The company at dinner was recruited by two cheerful couples – one of them the vicar and his wife, and by a silent young man who had come down to fish. This was a relief to Mr Coyle, who had begun to wonder what was after all expected of him and why he had been such a fool as to come, and who now felt that for the first hours at least the situation would not have directly to be dealt with. Indeed he found, as he had found before, sufficient occupation for his ingenuity in reading the various symptoms of which the picture before him was an expression. He should probably have an irritating day on the morrow: he foresaw the difficulty of the long decorous Sunday and how dry Jane Wingrave's ideas, elicited in a strenuous conference, would taste. She and her father would make him feel that they depended upon him for the impossible, and if they should try to associate him with a merely stupid policy he might end by telling them what he thought of it – an accident not required to make his visit a sensible mistake. The old man's actual design was evidently to let their friends see in it a positive mark of their being all right. The presence of the great London coach was tantamount to a profession of faith in the results of the impending examination. It had clearly been obtained from Owen, rather to Spencer Coyle's surprise, that he would do nothing to interfere with the apparent harmony. He let the allusions to his hard work pass and, holding his tongue about his affairs, talked to the ladies as amicably as if he had not been 'cut off'. When Spencer Coyle looked at him once or twice across the table, catching his eye, which showed an indefinable passion, he saw a puzzling pathos in his laughing face: one couldn't resist a pang for a young lamb so visibly marked for sacrifice. 'Hang him – what a pity he's such a fighter!' he privately sighed, with a want of logic that was only superficial.

This idea however would have absorbed him more if so much of his attention had not been given to Kate Julian, who now that he had her well before him struck him as a remarkable and even as a possibly fascinating young woman. The fascination resided not in any extraordinary prettiness, for if she was handsome, with her long Eastern eyes, her magnificent hair and her general unabashed originality, he had seen complexions rosier and features that pleased him more: it resided in a strange impression that she gave of being exactly the sort of person whom, in her position, common considerations, those of prudence and perhaps even a little those of decorum, would have enjoined on her not to be. She was what was vulgarly termed a dependant – penniless, patronized, tolerated; but something in her aspect and manner signified that if her situation was inferior, her spirit, to make up for it, was above precautions or submissions. It was not in the least that she was aggressive, she was too indifferent for that; it was only as if, having nothing either to gain or to lose, she could afford to do as she liked. It occurred to Spencer Coyle that she might really have had more at stake than her imagination appeared to take account of ; whatever it was at any rate he had never seen a young woman at less pains to be on the safe side. He wondered inevitably how the peace was kept between Jane Wingrave and such an inmate as this; but those questions of course were unfathomable deeps. Perhaps Kate Julian lorded it even over her protectress. The other time he was at Paramore he had received an impression that, with Sir Philip beside her, the girl could fight with her back to the wall. She amused Sir Philip, she charmed him, and he liked people who weren't afraid; between him and his daughter moreover there was no doubt which was the higher in command. Miss Wingrave took many things for granted, and most of all the rigour of discipline and the fate of the vanquished and the captive.

But between their clever boy and so original a companion of his childhood what odd relation would have grown up? It couldn't be indifference, and yet on the part of happy, handsome, youthful creatures it was still less likely to be aversion. They weren't Paul and Virginia, but they must have had their common summer and their idyll: no nice girl could have disliked such a nice fellow for anything but not liking her, and no nice fellow could have resisted such propinquity. Mr Coyle remembered indeed that Mrs Julian had spoken to him as if the propinquity had been by no means constant, owing to her daughter's absences at school, to say nothing of Owen's; her visits to a few friends who were so kind as to 'take her' from time to time; her sojourns in London – so difficult to manage, but still managed by God's help – for 'advantages', for drawing and singing, especially drawing or rather painting, in oils, in which she had had immense success. But the good lady had also mentioned that the young people were quite brother and sister, which was a little, after all, like Paul and Virginia. Mrs Coyle had been right, and it was apparent that Virginia was doing her best to make the time pass agreeably for young Lechmere. There was no such whirl of conversation as to render it an effort for Mr Coyle to reflect on these things, for the tone of the occasion, thanks principally to the other guests, was not disposed to stray – it tended to the repetition of anecdote and the discussion of rents, topics that huddled together like uneasy animals. He could judge how intensely his hosts wished the evening to pass off as if nothing had happened; and this gave him the measure of their private resentment. Before dinner was over he found himself fidgetty about his second pupil. Young Lechmere, since he began to cram, had done all that might have been expected of him; but this couldn't blind his instructor to a present perception of his being in moments of relaxation as innocent as a babe. Mr Coyle had considered that the amusements of Paramore would probably give him a fillip, and the poor fellow's manner testified to the soundness of the forecast. The fillip had been unmistakably administered; it had come in the form of a revelation. The light on young Lechmere's brow announced with a candour that was almost an appeal for compassion, or at least a deprecation of ridicule, that he had never seen anything like Miss Julian.

4

In the drawing-room after dinner the girl found an occasion to approach Spencer Coyle. She stood before him a moment, smiling while she opened and shut her fan, and then she said abruptly, raising her strange eyes: "I know what you've come for, but it isn't any use."

"I've come to look after you a little. Isn't that any use?"

"It's very kind. But I'm not the question of the hour. You won't do anything with Owen."

Spencer Coyle hesitated a moment. "What will you do with his young friend?"

She stared, looked round her.

"Mr Lechmere? Oh, poor little lad! We've been talking about Owen. He admires him so."

"So do I. I should tell you that."

"So do we all. That's why we're in such despair."

"Personally then you'd like him to be a soldier?" Spencer Coyle inquired.

"I've quite set my heart on it. I adore the army and I'm awfully fond of my old playmate," said Miss Julian.

Her interlocutor remembered the young man's own different version of her attitude; but he judged it loyal not to challenge the girl.

"It's not conceivable that your old playmate shouldn't be fond of you. He must therefore wish to please you; and I don't see why – between you – you don't set the matter right."

"Wish to please me!" Miss Julian exclaimed. "I'm sorry

to say he shows no such desire. He thinks me an impudent wretch. I've told him what I think of him, and he simply hates me."

"But you think so highly! You just told me you admire him."

"His talents, his possibilities, yes; even his appearance, if I may allude to such a matter. But I don't admire his present behaviour."

"Have you had the question out with him?" Spencer Coyle asked.

"Oh, yes, I've ventured to be frank – the occasion seemed to excuse it. He couldn't like what I said."

"What did you say?"

Miss Julian, thinking a moment, opened and shut her fan again.

"Why, that such conduct isn't that of a gentleman!"

After she had spoken her eyes met Spencer Coyle's, who looked into their charming depths.

"Do you want then so much to send him off to be killed?"

"How odd for you to ask that – in such a way!" she replied with a laugh. "I don't understand your position: I thought your line was to make soldiers!"

"You should take my little joke. But, as regards Owen Wingrave, there's no 'making' needed," Mr Coyle added. "To my sense" – the little crammer paused a moment, as if with a consciousness of responsibility for his paradox – "to my sense he is, in a high sense of the term, a fighting man."

"Ah, let him prove it!" the girl exclaimed, turning away.

Spencer Coyle let her go; there was something in her tone that annoyed and even a little shocked him. There had evidently been a violent passage between these young people, and the reflection that such a matter was after all none of his business only made him more sore. It was indeed a military house, and she was at any rate a person who placed her ideal of manhood (young persons doubtless always had their ideals of manhood) in the type of the belted warrior. It was a taste like another; but, even a quarter of an hour later, finding himself near young Lechmere, in whom this type was embodied, Spencer Coyle was still so ruffled that he addressed the innocent lad with a certain magisterial dryness. "You're not to sit up late, you know. That's not what I brought you down for." The dinner-guests were taking leave and the bedroom candles twinkled in a monitory row. Young Lechmere however was too agreeably agitated to be accessible to a snub: he had a happy pre-occupation which almost engendered a grin.

"I'm only too eager for bedtime. Do you know there's an awfully jolly room?"

"Surely they haven't put you there?"

"No indeed: no one has passed a night in it for ages. But that's exactly what I want to do – it would be tremendous fun."

"And have you been trying to get Miss Julian's permission?"

"Oh, she can't give leave, she says. But she believes in it, and she maintains that no man dare."

"No man shall! A man in your critical position in

particular must have a quiet night," said Spencer Coyle.

Young Lechmere gave a disappointed but reasonable sigh.

"Oh, all right. But mayn't I sit up for a little go at Wingrave? I haven't had any yet."

Mr Coyle looked at his watch.

"You may smoke one cigarette."

He felt a hand on his shoulder, and he turned round to see his wife tilting candle-grease upon his coat. The ladies were going to bed and it was Sir Philip's inveterate hour; but Mrs Coyle confided to her husband that after the dreadful things he had told her she positively declined to be left alone, for no matter how short an interval, in any part of the house. He promised to follow her within three minutes, and after the orthodox handshakes the ladies rustled away. The forms were kept up at Paramore as bravely as if the old house had no present heartache. The only one of which Spencer Coyle noticed the omission was some salutation to himself from Kate Julian. She gave him neither a word nor a glance, but he saw her look hard at Owen Wingrave. Her mother, timid and pitying, was apparently the only person from whom this young man caught an inclination of the head. Miss Wingrave marshalled the three ladies – her little procession of twinkling tapers – up the wide oaken stairs and past the watching portrait of her ill-fated ancestor. Sir Philip's servant appeared and offered his arm to the old man, who turned a perpendicular back on poor Owen when the boy made a vague movement to anticipate this office. Spencer Coyle learned afterwards that before Owen had forfeited favour it had always, when he was at home, been his privilege at bedtime to conduct his grandfather ceremoniously to rest. Sir Philip's habits were contemptuously different now. His apartments were on the lower floor and he shuffled stiffly off to them with his valet's help, after fixing for a moment significantly on the most responsible of his visitors the thick red ray, like the glow of stirred embers, that always made his eyes conflict oddly with his mild manners. They seemed to say to Spencer Coyle 'We'll let the young scoundrel have it to-morrow!' One might have gathered from them that the young scoundrel, who had now strolled to the other end of the hall, had at least forged a cheque. Mr Coyle watched him an instant, saw him drop nervously into a chair and then with a restless movement get up. The same movement brought him back to where his late instructor stood addressing a last injunction to young Lechmere.

"I'm going to bed and I should like you particularly to conform to what I said to you a short time ago. Smoke a single cigarette with your friend here and then go to your room. You'll have me down on you if I hear of your having, during the night, tried any preposterous games." Young Lechmere, looking down with his hands in his pockets, said nothing – he only poked at the corner of a rug with his toe; so that Spencer Coyle, dissatisfied with so tacit a pledge, presently went on, to Owen: "I must request you, Wingrave, not to keep this sensitive subject sitting up – and indeed to put him to bed and turn his key in the door." As Owen

stared an instant, apparently not understanding the motive
of so much solicitude, he added: "Lechmere has a morbid
curiosity about one of your legends – of your historic rooms.
Nip it in the bud."

"Oh, the legend's rather good, but I'm afraid the room's
an awful sell!" Owen laughed.

"You know you don't believe that, my boy!" young
Lechmere exclaimed.

"I don't think he does," said Mr Coyle, noticing Owen's
mottled flush.

"He wouldn't try a night there himself!" young Lechmere
pursued.

"I know who told you that," rejoined Owen, lighting
a cigarette in an embarrassed way at the candle, without
offering one to either of his companions.

"Well, what if she did?" asked the younger of these
gentlemen, rather red. "Do you want them all yourself?" he
continued facetiously, fumbling in the cigarette-box.

Owen Wingrave only smoked quietly; then he exclaimed:
"Yes – what if she did? But she doesn't know," he added.

"She doesn't know what?"

"She doesn't know anything! – I'll tuck him in!" Owen
went on gaily to Mr Coyle, who saw that his presence, now
that a certain note had been struck, made the young men
uncomfortable. He was curious, but there was a kind of
discretion, with his pupils, that he had always pretended to
practise; a discretion that however didn't prevent him as he
took his way upstairs from recommending them not to be

donkeys.

At the top of the staircase, to his surprise, he met Miss Julian, who was apparently going down again. She had not begun to undress, nor was she perceptibly disconcerted at seeing him. She nevertheless, in a manner slightly at variance with the rigour with which she had overlooked him ten minutes before, dropped the words: "I'm going down to look for something. I've lost a jewel."

"A jewel?"

"A rather good turquoise, out of my locket. As it's the only ornament I have the honour to possess—!" And she passed down.

"Shall I go with you and help you?" asked Spencer Coyle.

The girl paused a few steps below him, looking back with her Oriental eyes.

"Don't I hear voices in the hall?"

"Those remarkable young men are there."

"They'll help me." And Kate Julian descended.

Spencer Coyle was tempted to follow her, but remembering his standard of tact he rejoined his wife in their apartment. He delayed however to go to bed, and though he went into his dressing-room he couldn't bring himself even to take off his coat. He pretended for half an hour to read a novel; after which, quietly, or perhaps I should say agitatedly, he passed from the dressing-room into the corridor. He followed this passage to the door of the room which he knew to have been assigned to young Lechmere and was comforted to see that it was closed. Half an hour earlier he had seen it standing open; therefore he could take for granted that the bewildered boy had come to bed. It was of this he had wished to assure himself, and having done so he was on the point of retreating. But at the same instant he heard a sound in the room – the occupant was doing, at the window, something which showed him that he might knock without the reproach of waking his pupil up. Young Lechmere came in fact to the door in his shirt and trousers. He admitted his visitor in some surprise, and when the door was closed again Spencer Coyle said:

"I don't want to make your life a burden to you, but I had it on my conscience to see for myself that you're not exposed to undue excitement."

"Oh, there's plenty of that!" said the ingenuous youth. "Miss Julian came down again."

"To look for a turquoise?"

"So she said."

"Did she find it?"

"I don't know. I came up. I left her with poor Wingrave."

"Quite the right thing," said Spencer Coyle.

"I don't know," young Lechmere repeated uneasily. "I left them quarrelling."

"What about?"

"I don't understand. They're a quaint pair!"

Spencer Coyle hesitated. He had, fundamentally, principles and scruples, but what he had in particular just now was a curiosity, or rather, to recognise it for what it was, a sympathy, which brushed them away.

"Does it strike you that she's down on him?" he permitted himself to inquire.

"Rather! – when she tells him he lies!"

"What do you mean?"

"Why, before me. It made me leave them; it was getting too hot. I stupidly brought up the question of the haunted room again, and said how sorry I was that I had had to promise you not to try my luck with it."

"You can't pry about in that gross way in other people's houses – you can't take such liberties, you know!" Mr Coyle interjected.

"I'm all right – see how good I am. I don't want to go near the place!" said young Lechmere, confidingly. "Miss Julian said to me 'Oh, I daresay you'd risk it, but' – and she turned and laughed at poor Owen – 'that's more than we can expect of a gentleman who has taken his extraordinary line.' I could see that something had already passed between them on the subject – some teasing or challenging of hers. It may have been only chaff, but his chucking the profession had evidently brought up the question of his pluck."

"And what did Owen say?"

"Nothing at first; but presently he brought out very quietly: 'I spent all last night in the confounded place.' We both stared and cried out at this and I asked him what he had seen there. He said he had seen nothing, and Miss Julian replied that he ought to tell his story better than that – he ought to make something good of it. 'It's not a story – it's a simple fact,' said he; on which she jeered at him and wanted to know why, if he had done it, he hadn't told her in the morning, since he knew what she thought of him. 'I know, but I don't care,' said Wingrave. This made her angry, and she asked him quite seriously whether he would care if he should know she believed him to be trying to deceive us."

"Ah, what a brute!" cried Spencer Coyle.

"She's a most extraordinary girl – I don't know what she's up to."

"Extraordinary indeed – to be romping and bandying words at that hour of the night with fast young men!"

Young Lechmere reflected a moment. "I mean because I think she likes him."

Spencer Coyle was so struck with this unwonted symptom of subtlety that he flashed out: "And do you think he likes her?"

But his interlocutor only replied with a puzzled sigh and a plaintive "I don't know – I give it up! – I'm sure he did see something or hear something," young Lechmere added.

"In that ridiculous place? What makes you sure?"

"I don't know – he looks as if he had. He behaves as if he had."

"Why then shouldn't he mention it?"

Young Lechmere thought a moment. "Perhaps it's too gruesome!"

Spencer Coyle gave a laugh. "Aren't you glad then you're not in it?"

"Uncommonly!"

"Go to bed, you goose," said Spencer Coyle, with another

laugh. "But before you go tell me what he said when she told him he was trying to deceive you."

" 'Take me there yourself, then, and lock me in!' "

"And did she take him?"

"I don't know – I came up."

Spencer Coyle exchanged a long look with his pupil.

"I don't think they're in the hall now. Where's Owen's own room?"

"I haven't the least idea."

Mr Coyle was perplexed; he was in equal ignorance, and he couldn't go about trying doors. He bade young Lechmere sink to slumber, and came out into the passage. He asked himself if he should be able to find his way to the room Owen had formerly shown him, remembering that in common with many of the others it had its ancient name painted upon it. But the corridors of Paramore were intricate; moreover some of the servants would still be up, and he didn't wish to have the appearance of roaming over the house. He went back to his own quarters, where Mrs Coyle soon perceived that his inability to rest had not subsided. As she confessed for her own part, in the dreadful place, to an increased sense of 'creepiness', they spent the early part of the night in conversation, so that a portion of their vigil was inevitably beguiled by her husband's account of his colloquy with little Lechmere and by their exchange of opinions upon it. Toward two o'clock Mrs Coyle became so nervous about their persecuted young friend, and so possessed by the fear that that wicked girl had availed herself of his invitation to

put him to an abominable test, that she begged her husband
to go and look into the matter at whatever cost to his own
equilibrium. But Spencer Coyle, perversely, had ended,
as the perfect stillness of the night settled upon them, by
charming himself into a tremulous acquiescence in Owen's
readiness to face a formidable ordeal – an ordeal the more
formidable to an excited imagination as the poor boy now
knew from the experience of the previous night how resolute
an effort he should have to make. "I hope he is there," he said
to his wife: "it puts them all so in the wrong!" At any rate
he couldn't take upon himself to explore a house he knew
so little. He was inconsequent – he didn't prepare for bed.
He sat in the dressing-room with his light and his novel,
waiting to find himself nodding. At last however Mrs Coyle
turned over and ceased to talk, and at last too he fell asleep
in his chair. How long he slept he only knew afterwards by
computation; what he knew to begin with was that he had
started up, in confusion, with the sense of a sudden appalling
sound. His sense cleared itself quickly, helped doubtless by a
confirmatory cry of horror from his wife's room. But he gave
no heed to his wife; he had already bounded into the passage.
There the sound was repeated – it was the "Help! help!" of a
woman in agonised terror. It came from a distant quarter of
the house, but the quarter was sufficiently indicated. Spencer
Coyle rushed straight before him, with the sound of opening
doors and alarmed voices in his ears and the faintness of the
early dawn in his eyes. At a turn of one of the passages he
came upon the white figure of a girl in a swoon on a bench,

and in the vividness of the revelation he read as he went that Kate Julian, stricken in her pride too late with a chill of compunction for what she had mockingly done, had, after coming to release the victim of her derision, reeled away, overwhelmed, from the catastrophe that was her work – the catastrophe that the next moment he found himself aghast at on the threshold of an open door. Owen Wingrave, dressed as he had last seen him, lay dead on the spot on which his ancestor had been found. He looked like a young soldier on a battle-field.

THE END

Lightning Source UK Ltd.
Milton Keynes UK
UKOW042223150413

209269UK00004B/909/P